DIARY OF

SUPER
SWIMMER

Shamini Flint

Illustrated by Sally Heinrich

ALLEN&UNWIN
SYDNEY·MELBOURNE·AUCKLAND·LONDON

This edition published in 2014

First published in Singapore in 2013 by Sunbear Publishing

Allen & Unwin
83 Alexander Street
Crows Nest NSW 2065
Australia
Phone: (612) 8425 0100
Fax: (612) 9906 2218
Email: info@allenandunwin.com
Web: www.allenandunwin.com

A Cataloguing-in-Publication entry is available
from the National Library of Australia
www.trove.nla.gov.au

ISBN 978 1 74331 884 3

Text design by Sally Heinrich
Series cover concept by Jaime Harrison
Set in 12¾/14 pt Comic Sans

This book was printed in March 2014 at Griffin Press,
168 Cross Keys Road, Salisbury South, South Australia 5106, Australia.
www.griffinpress.com.au

10 9 8 7 6 5 4 3 2

About the Author

Shamini Flint lives in Singapore with her husband and two children. She is an ex-lawyer, ex-lecturer, stay-at-home mum and writer. She loves swimming!

www.shaminiflint.com

MY SWIMMING DIARY

Dad wants me to swim.

Dad wants me to SWIM!

DAD WANTS ME TO SWIM!!!

Do I look like a fish?

Or a turtle?

Or a duck?

Maybe a little
bit like a duck.

Gemma

That's not funny, Gemma.

My sister Gemma likes to write notes
in my diaries.

I've tried to hide the diaries.

But she always finds them.

Mind you, I've thought of a really good spot to hide my diary this time. Gemma will never find it.

I'll wrap it in plastic ...

and lock it in a treasure chest ...

find a shipwreck ...

and hide it there ... deep under the sea!

NOT!!!!

That's where I'd hide my diary if I could swim ...

BUT I CAN'T SWIM!!!

I'll love swimming exactly as much as I love ...

spinach for dinner ...

homework ...

or Hulk.

NOT AT ALL!!!

The problem is that Dad is convinced that I'm good at sport. I'm not.

We just haven't found the right sport, son!

We're more likely to find ...

the abominable snowman ...

or the lost city of Atlantis ...

Where are my glasses?

or Mum's missing reading glasses ...

than a sport I'm good at.

(All right, maybe not Mum's reading glasses. They're usually on her head.)

Eh? Why would I think inside the box?

Dad's written a book called *Pull Yourself Up by Your Own Bootstraps*. He's always quoting from it. It hasn't helped yet.

What have we tried so far?
Soccer, cricket, rugby ...

taekwondo and track and field ...

It's not a good sign if Dad is contradicting his own book.

Very funny. NOT!!!

Besides, I think Dad means I should try
water sports ...

Of all the dumb ideas in the history of the world, this must be the dumbest!

Dumber than trying to fly with a few feathers glued to your arms ...

Dumber than being friendly to a lion ...

Dumber than making fun of Hulk!!!

I've got you something that will help!

What could it be?

Floats?

A swimming noodle?

A life jacket?

It's a poster!

A poster?

KEEP CALM and CARRY ON

11

How about I 'keep calm and pretend I'm adopted'?

How about I 'keep calm and go into hiding'??

How about I 'keep calm and call the police'???

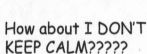

How about I DON'T KEEP CALM?????

To be very clear about it, my name in Marcus Atkinson. I am nine years old.

I don't want to SWIM.

NOT NOW. NOT EVER.

Big surprise.

We always need a coach.

None of my previous coaches have been happy
with me.

Maybe I should give the new guy my poster.

Actually, I've had swimming lessons before. At school. They didn't go so well.

Thank goodness! One normal guy.

So much for normal ...

Really? Think of the water as my home?

So where's the TV?

Or my Xbox?

Or dinner?

21

23

24

I think I will draw a curtain over what happened next.

After all, someone might read this diary some day.

That's not fair!

Gemma

I found out from Shark. He's in my class. Everyone's talking about it!!

You can guess what happened next.

Help!! Even more time in my room with a paper bag over my head!

If you can dream it, you can do it! Chapter 44.

Really, Dad?

Last night I dreamt I was Godzilla trampling through Tokyo ...

The night before, I dreamt I was sliding on rainbows ...

Last week, I dreamt that I climbed Mt Everest. Backwards. On stilts. While carrying a donkey on my head.

I know. That was a weird dream ...

Do you really think I can do any of that in real life??

SWIMMING LESSON NO. 1

Someone needs to tell Harriet. She's been doing it wrong all these months.

29

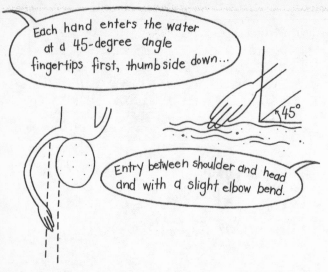

Eh? Seriously? How can putting my hand in water be so complicated?

I've managed cookie jars ...

the fridge ...

Gemma's schoolbag ...

What???

Just kidding ... GULP!

31

Then I tried arms and legs together.
That went well ... NOT!!

Let's hope I never have to outrun a shark ...

or a killer whale ...

or a sea serpent.

I'd be fish food.

Marcus 'Fish Food' Atkinson !!!

Thanks, guys ...

What can I say?

My life flashed before my eyes ...

I wondered if Dad would feel guilty ...

I wondered if Gemma would get my stuff ...

Of course!!

For a brief moment, I thought I could fly ...

I couldn't ...

Whenever I need to sink straight to the bottom of the swimming pool and sit there, I'll be fine.

BECAUSE that's all I'm WORKING ON!!!

41

It's true that Harriet loves water.

She splashes ...

she thrashes ...

she blows bubbles ...

sigh...

I complained to my friends.

Only Lizzie from soccer was sympathetic ...

I might have guessed. Lizzie only cares about soccer ...

If she could only rescue a single thing from a burning building, she'd leave ...

the Mona Lisa ...

a huge bag of money ...

the Kohinoor diamond ...

and rescue her football.

SWIMMING LESSON NO. 2

I splashed water up my nose - that's what happened!!

48

49

I wasn't much good at water polo as I had to hold on to the sides the whole time. Otherwise, I'd just sink to the bottom.

Finally, Coach gave me floats.

I'm really not sure life can get much worse than this ...

What?? Has Mum written her own book now?
I'll like it if I keep trying?

Does that mean that
someday I'll like ...

arm-wrestling Hulk ...

spelling tests ...

Gemma ...

if I keep trying???

Maybe swimming might come in useful some day if ...

I'm stuck on a desert
island ...

or being chased by
an octopus ...

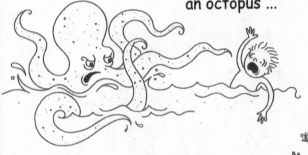

or falling out of a helicopter
into a lake ...

56

From now on I'm going to ...

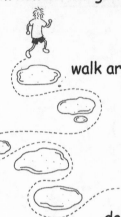

walk around puddles ...

dodge raindrops ...

and NEVER bathe again!!

Never say never!
Gemma

ARGGGHHHHHHHH!!

SWIMMING LESSON NO. 3

The butterfly?

We're learning to perch on flowers?

We're learning to flap our wings gaily?

We're learning to flit about in the sunshine?

That's a bit weird.

But it's better than swimming so count me in!

59

61

Like a dolphin?
I thought this stroke was called the butterfly?

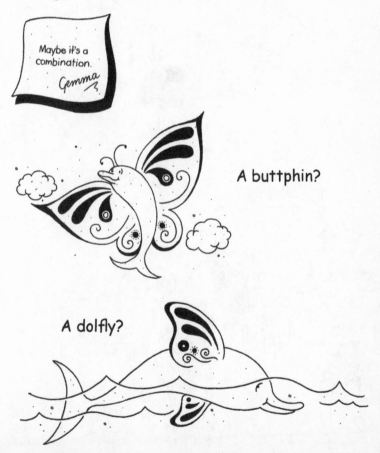

A buttphin?

A dolfly?

64

For the last time, I'm HUMAN.

Not a butterfly or dolphin or shark or frog!!

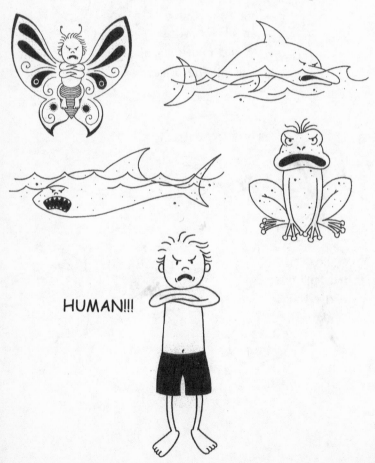

HUMAN!!!

Later Dad told me they were three of the greatest swimmers of all time.

They must all be a different sort of human ... SIGH!!!

68

FIRST RACE

I guess that makes sense. It's the only stroke where I actually stayed above water ...

Life is a race? Life is a race where we all end up dead in the end??

Thanks, Dad. That's made me feel a lot better. NOT.

72

73

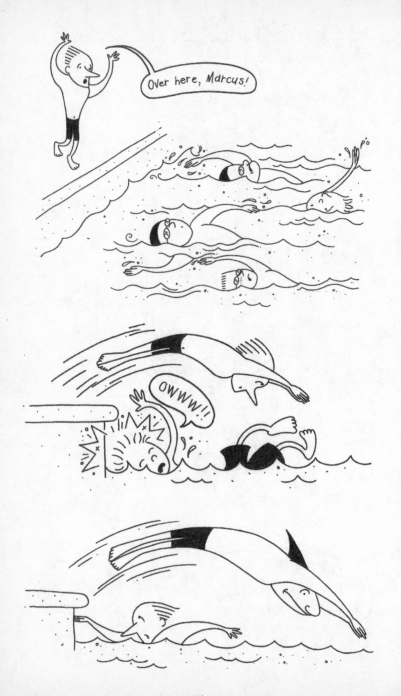

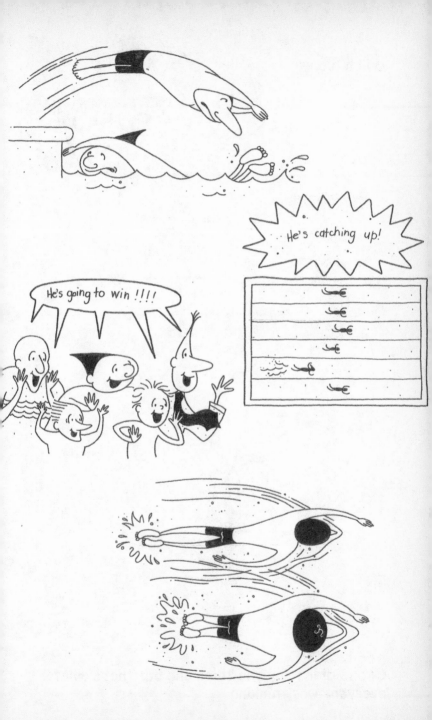

Dolph did it!!!

Ok, he didn't say the third one but that's what everyone was thinking.

I'm not on the ladder to success, Dad, I'm on the slippery snake to failure ...

I'm on a lonely road to nowhere ...

I've got a one way ticket to Planet Loser ...

Dad has a point. Gemma's never been interested in sports before.

Woof! Woof!

You're right, Spot. Both my sisters are better swimmers than me. SIGH...

Hey Marcus! I have a surprise!

It's my birthday?

We're going on holiday?

We're having pizza for dinner?

Yes, Dad. I love the surprise. NOT.

I tried to reason with
him one last time.

There are only three
things I could do ...

I'll have to join an
expedition to the
Amazon ...

I'll have to become a lonely
cowboy in the Wild West ...

I'll have to turn to a life of crime ...

Whatever happens,
I can't stay here!!

Just for once, Gemma was right.

Hey!
I'm always
right.

I'm going to have to swim.

I'm going to have to swim the crawl!!

I'm going to have to swim the anchor leg!

I'M GOING TO COME LAST AGAIN!!

I'M GOING TO BE DISQUALIFIED!!!

ARRRGGGHHHHHHH!!!

Maybe I can teach you to swim.

Gemma

Yeah, right.

And while you're at it, why don't you teach me to ...

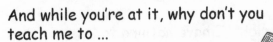

build a spaceship with toothpicks?

Or write a book blindfolded?

Or become a trapeze artist?

OR ANY OTHER IMPOSSIBLE THING!!!

She's right. I have nothing to lose.

All right, I'll give it a shot.

It's a big, watery monster and it's after me!
This is going to be harder than I thought...
Let's begin by floating.
On your back...
like this...

RACE DAY

Well, Gemma's taught me to swim ... sort of.

I do a part crawl, part doggie paddle, part panic attack ...

And I can get exactly half way across the pool.

Gemma thinks that when I'm racing, I'll manage to get to the end.

Not going to happen.

I'm going to get to the middle of the pool and then coach is going to have to pull me out by my shorts.

HELP!!!

There are six teams competing. Some of them also have the new cool kit.

I wonder whether that means they have a really rubbish player swimming the anchor leg too.
I doubt it.

That's good to know. In this case, I invented the aeroplane ...

 used it to fly across the Pacific Ocean ...

parachuted into a swimming pool ...

and won three Olympic gold medals for swimming.

What's happening to my world? Now complete strangers are being mean to me?

And that's when I had my idea.

A GREAT IDEA!!

THE GREATEST
IDEA THAT ANY
HUMAN BEING HAD
EVER HAD!!

Dad is right!
Greatness is in
the mind ...

The teams lined up.

Barry was swimming the backstroke.

He got off to a
good start.

But the other teams
were good ...

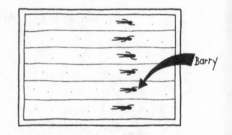

Barry

He couldn't get away
from them.

It was neck and neck.

Come on, Barry!

Dolph dived in ...

A perfect breaststroke. I really wish I could swim like that.

We were in the lead now.

I was feeling confident.

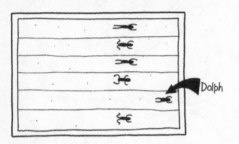

No one is better than Shark at the butterfly.

Hulk IS better than Shark at the butterfly!

I can't believe it ...

Hulk is in the lead!

Shark is doing his best ...

But he's behind by five metres.

It's all up to the anchor leg!

107

111

Errrr ... so who's that??

116

118

Have you read my Rugby Diary ...

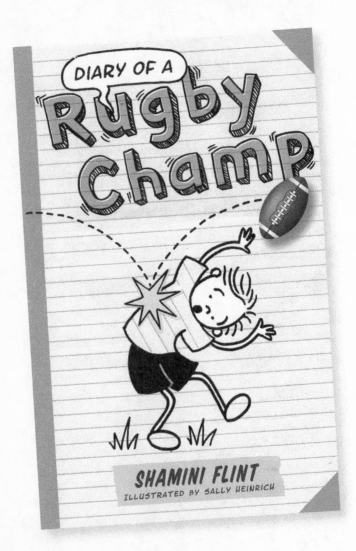

Or my Cricket Diary?

What about my Soccer Diary?

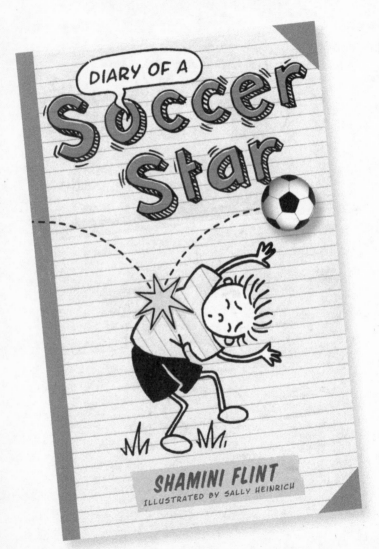

Or my Taekwondo Diary?

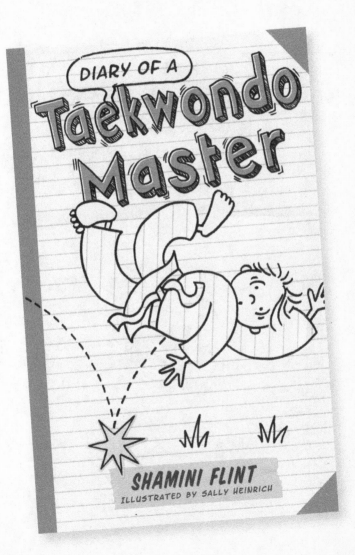

And then there's my Track and Field Diary ...

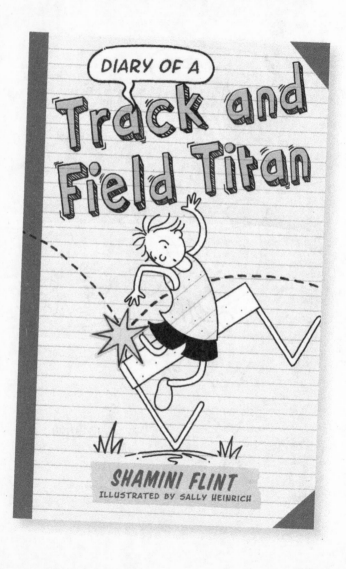

DIARY OF A

Track and Field Titan

SHAMINI FLINT
ILLUSTRATED BY SALLY HEINRICH